WEiRDO

CRAZY WEIRD!

6

Scholastic Press
345 Pacific Highway Lindfield NSW 2070
An imprint of Scholastic Australia Pty Limited (ABN 11 000 614 577)
PO Box 579 Gosford NSW 2250
www.scholastic.com.au

Part of the Scholastic Group
Sydney • Auckland • New York • Toronto • London • Mexico City
• New Delhi • Hong Kong • Buenos Aires • Puerto Rico

First published by Scholastic Australia in 2016.
Text copyright © Anh Do, 2016.
Illustrations copyright © Jules Faber, 2016.

National Library of Australia Cataloguing-in-Publication entry
Creator: Do, Anh, author.
Title: WeirDo 6 / Anh Do; Jules Faber.
ISBN: 9781760159085 (paperback)
9781760278380 (book club edition)
Series: Do, Anh. WeirDo; 6.
Target Audience: For primary school age.
Subjects: Children's stories.
Other Creators/Contributors:
Faber, Jules, 1971-, illustrator.
Dewey Number: A823.4

Typeset in Grenadine MVB, Push Ups and Lunch Box.

Printed by RR Donnelley.
Scholastic Australia's policy, in association with
RR Donnelley, is to use papers that are renewable and made
efficiently from wood grown in responsibly managed forests,
so as to minimise its environmental footprint.

20 19 18 17 16 15   19 20 / 1

BLAH,
BLAH,
BLAH

ANH DO

Illustrated by JULES FABER

WEiRDO 6
CRAZY WEIRD!

A SCHOLASTIC PRESS BOOK
FROM SCHOLASTIC AUSTRALIA

I wasn't **at all** scared about seeing the **dentist**...

not scared

...until I heard the **drilling**!

DRRRRRRRRRRRRRRR

a little
bit scared

RRRRRRRRRR!

Oh no!

And then the **crying** started!

PLEASE! SOMEBODY SAVE ME

'Don't worry,' said Granddad. 'You can always borrow **my teeth** if you need to!'

HERE YOU GO!

I thought about it for a second. If I wore Granddad's teeth, the dentist could **drill** all he wanted and **it wouldn't hurt at all!**

But the sight of **all that slobber** put me off.

UM, NO, THANKS.

DRRRRRRRR!

Then the drilling got **even louder**! It was like a **jackhammer**!

What was going on in there?!

THIS MIGHT HURT A LITTLE . . .

I didn't want **any** drills **anywhere near** my teeth!

I ran to the window to **escape**!

When I looked down, I realised that the jackhammering was coming from **across the street!**

DRRRRRRRRRRRRRRRRRR!

It was just a worker jackhammering **the road**!

Phew!

But what about the **crying**?

PLEASE, SOMEBODY SAVE ME FROM THIS GIANT HOT DOG!

The **crying** had been coming from the **telly**!

A man in a white coat walked into the waiting room. He looked at his clipboard and **chuckled**.

WEIR . . . DO?

'That's me,' I said and stood up.

'Weir Do. That's a funny name,' he said with a toothy grin.

A dentist called **Phil McCavity**!? Fill. My. Cavity. And he thinks **I've** got a funny name?

The dentist's chair was **really** cool. It moved up and down like a robot.

SIT. DOWN.

There were all these **weird little tool** things lined up on a tray. Like a little **stick with a mirror** on the end of it.

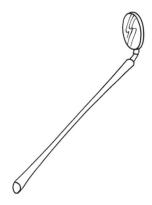

That'd be **pretty cool** for sneaking around corners.

If you were a mouse.

UH-OH!

Then there was another **stick with a claw** thing on the end of it.

That'd be handy for reaching things that are just a bit **too high**.

REALLY GOOD CHIPS

GOT IT!

And there was this **mini vacuum cleaner** thing that the nurse stuck into the corner of my mouth to **suck**

out

spit!

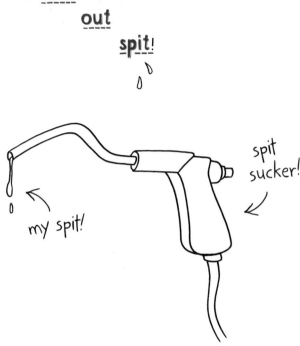

my spit!

spit sucker!

It was **gross.** I'd hate to be the person who has to empty **that vacuum bag**!

Dr Phil took a good look around in my mouth.

'Open **wider**, please,' he said.

So I opened **wider**.

'Just a **little w-i-d-e-r**,' he said.

So I opened my mouth as **w-i-d-e** as I could.

'Even w -i -d -e -r.'

Even w -i -d -e -r? What does he think I am? **A snake?**

'How are you today?' the dentist asked.

'Very well, thanks,' I **tried** to say.

But it came out sounding like—

ORRA
BORRA
BURRA!

The funny thing was that Dr Phil seemed to know **exactly** what I was saying! I guess dentists get used to hearing people talk with their **mouths full.**

OOYA OOYA ICKLE ECKLE OCKLE!
YOU'RE RIGHT, WEIR. PETER PIPER DID PICK A PECK OF PICKLED PEPPERS.

'Well, Weir, the good news is that we don't need to pull out any teeth,' the dentist told me.

Hooray! Looks like I was worried for nothing! This dentist thing is easy peasy!

'However, you do need braces,' he said.

BRACES?!? I remembered a kid from my old school who had those.

Max Gribble. He called himself . . .

Max DRIBBLE!

He could barely close his mouth over those things! And that meant he **DRIBBLED ALL THE TIME** and **SPAT** all over you whenever he said something.

We quickly found ways to stay dry.

But my family didn't have raincoats at home. If I had braces and **spat** _everywhere_, Mum would probably make everyone wear **garbage bags** and **buckets**!

WHAT'S FOR DINNER?

SPIT ROAST.

'Don't worry, Weir,' said Dr Phil. 'You'll only need to wear the braces for a couple of months.'

A **couple of months**?
I was weird enough already,
without having a **mouth
full of metal** for
two months!

Oh man …

'Let's get started, shall we?' said the dentist.

'Maybe ... um, maybe we should wait a few weeks,' I stuttered. 'I think I can feel my teeth getting **straighter**

by

themselves!'

But Dr Phil **was not** convinced.

CHAPTER 2

The braces felt **really weird**. And I was sure they **looked** really weird, **too**. Maybe if I kept my mouth shut for two months, no-one would ever have to see them!

I'd just have to make sure I never **smiled**, **talked**, **ate** or **laughed** in public. How hard could that be?

'Give us a look,' said Sally.

But I just shook my head.

'I had to wear braces when I was a kid,' said
Mum. 'They were **really big** back then.
You should have seen me try to make it through
a metal detector!'

WHOOP! WHOOP!
WHOOP!

'I wore braces, too,' said Dad. 'But I had a **braces HELMET**! It was **enormous**!'

'It was **so huge**, I was always bumping into things.'

SQUAWK!

'And if anyone ever called me **"train tracks"**, I'd just laugh and play along.'

CHUGGA-CHUGGA,

CHUGGA-CHUGGA,

CHEW, CHEW!

HAHAHAHAHAHAHA!

'In fact, I made braces look **cool**,' said Dad.

SO GROOVY!

'And before long, **all** the kids in school wanted braces helmets! Like mine!'

Maybe it wasn't going to be so bad, I thought to myself.

'Come on,' said Sally. 'Give us a look.'

But I still wasn't ready to show anyone.

HUMMPPHH.

'Go on,' said Granddad.

HUMMPPHH.

'Do it! Do it!' said Blockhead.

'Woof!' added FiDo. 'Woof, woof!'

That's when Roger started **breakdancing** ...

WEE!

WEE! WEE! WEE!

He **STILL** can't say **WEIR**! It makes me laugh every time!

HAHA!
HAHA!
HAHA!

SQUAWK!

Suddenly, there was a huge **SQUAWK**!

I looked across at Blockhead and FiDo.

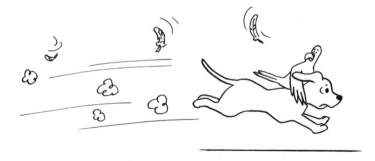

What was wrong?!

Oh no! Was it me?

Was it me they were scared of? My braces!?

'It's okay, Weir,' said Mum. 'They just need some time to get used to the **new** you!'

But it wasn't okay! My pets were **scared** of me! How bad did I look?!

How was everyone going to react at school tomorrow?

We were all going to the Fun Fair. It was meant to be **heaps** of fun—I'd been looking forward to it for weeks! But now I felt like I belonged in the sideshow alley, where people would come and stare at my **strange** face!

STEP RIGHT UP FOLKS, AND SEE THE BOY WHO LOOKS LIKE HE'S SWALLOWED A TOOLBOX!

Something tells me tomorrow is going to be a

loooooooooooooooooooooong day.

CHAPTER 3

It was hard getting used to having braces. I went through **22 toothbrushes** in the morning!

ARGH!

Luckily, Mum buys them in bulk.

I made it all the way onto the bus to the Fair without **anyone** seeing my braces. Not even *Bella*.

HI, WEIR!

HUMMF.

Bella and Henry had saved a seat for me, but I sat up the back of the bus in between **James Nott** and **Toby Hogan**, instead.

HUH?

It was **really** hard keeping quiet next to Toby Hogan. He kept showing me these football cards that he'd **drawn funny things on**.

'Look how I made this guy's ears bigger,' said Toby.

HAHAHAHAHA!

But I couldn't open my mouth and laugh!

Toby held up another card. 'And look what I did to this guy's eyebrows.'

HAHAHAHAHA!

He pulled out one last card.

'This is the best one of all,' he said. 'Look what I did to this guy's teeth!'

braces . . .

HAHAHAHAHA!

When we arrived at the Fair, guess where Henry wanted to go first?

LET'S GO CHECK OUT THE FUNHOUSE!

Not the **Funhouse**! It's impossible **not to laugh** in the Funhouse!

'Have **fun** in there, boys,' said Miss Franklin.

SEE YOU SOON!

We headed up the stairs and walked over a wobbly bridge. A **really** wobbly bridge!

I think someone should have told Henry that a **really wobbly bridge** is **NOT** the best place to eat an ice-cream.

WHOA!

Henry had ice-cream **ALL OVER HIS FACE**.
It was **SO** funny. I did my best again <u>**not**</u> to laugh.

HAHA!
HAHA!

me, trying
not to laugh!

When Hans Some, the **best-looking kid at
school**, walked across the wobbly bridge,
he didn't lose his balance once!

Totally . . .

← totally . . .

totally cool!

I made it over the **wobbly** bridge in a couple of big leaps, but nearly fell at the end!

LEAP, LEAP, HMMMPH!

Once we were all across...

we rode down a

HUGE SLIPPERY DIP!

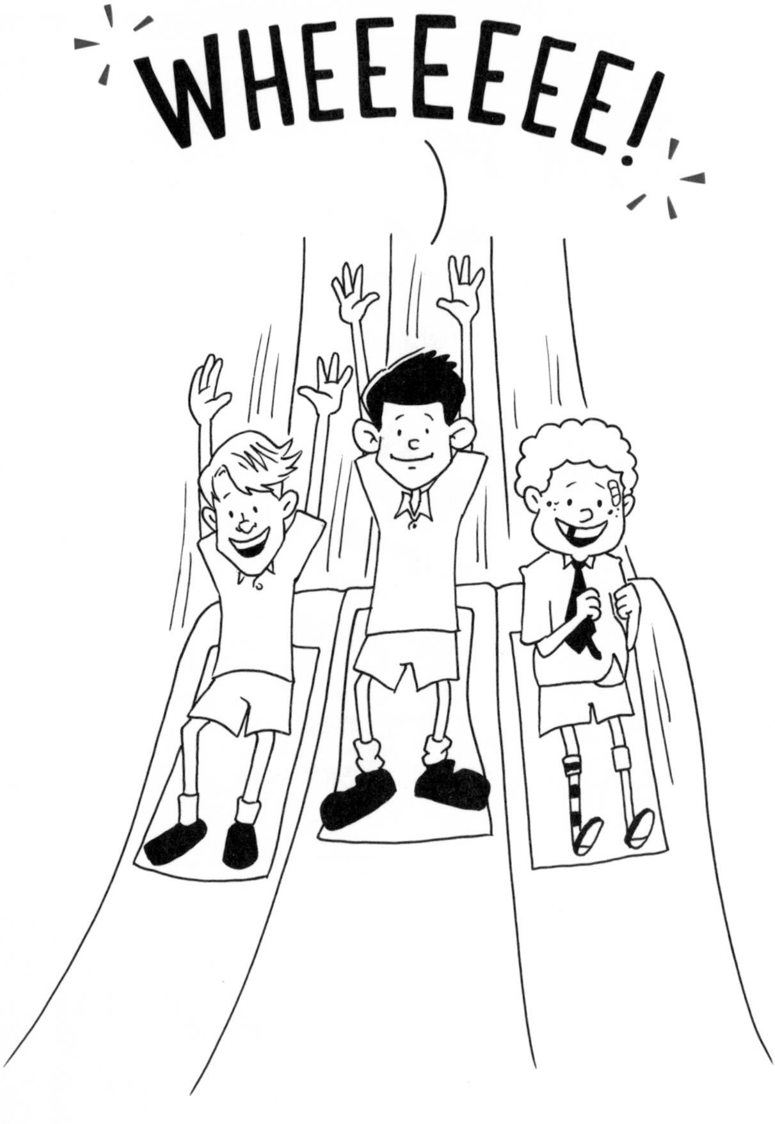
WHEEEEEE!

It was fun! I felt like a penguin sliding down an iceberg!

WELL, I'D RATHER BE SLIDING DOWN A SLIPPERY DIP!

ME TOO!

ICEBERGS FREEZE YOUR BUTT!

After the **giant slippery dip**, we made our way to the **Crazy Maze**.

The **Crazy Maze** was filled with all sorts of mirrors.

We walked through lots of twists and turns, and finally came to this big wall of weird mirrors.

Henry stepped up first and pulled a face.

In the mirrors, Henry looked **ten times** as <u>funny</u>!

Hans Some stepped up next.

Totally, totally, totally, totally, totally, totally, totally, totally, totally, **totally cool**.

Hans looked **ten times** as **handsome!**

When it was **my turn** to face the mirrors, I tried **really hard** not to smile and open my mouth ...

but then Toby Hogan appeared

out
of
nowhere . . .

and suddenly there were

TEN lots of bum cracks!

I couldn't help but laugh at that!

And then I saw **ten mouths full of braces!**

ARRRRRRRRGHHH

It was **terrible**! I had to get away! So I ran!
But I kept running into even **crazier** mirrors!

A **crazy wavy** one!

ARRRRRRR-
RGHHHHHHH-
HHHHHHHH!

HHHHHHHHHHHHH!

A **crazy tall** one!

ARRRRRRR-
RGHHHHHHH-
HHHHHHHH!

A **crazy short** one!

ARRRRRRR-
RGHHHHHHH-
HHHHHHHH!

And **every single time**, all I could see was
BRACES! I couldn't wait to get out of there!

I was outside catching my breath when I heard **Bella call out** to me.

WEIR!

'Weir, over here!' she called.

Oh no! I couldn't face Bella like this, so I had to act fast.

I had two choices—come up with a **clever story** that explained why I couldn't open my mouth ... or run away.

So I **ran away. ⟩⟩⟩⟩**

WHY IS WEIR AVOIDING ME?

CHAPTER 4

Henry and Hans finally caught up with me, and we wandered over to play some games.

We stopped at the **Carnival Clowns** first. Henry bought five ping pong balls and popped one into the mouth of the first clown in line.

But the clown suddenly coughed and spat the ball back out!

It was a **REAL CLOWN** just having a break!

Some of the other kids from our class were playing games, too.

Blake Green was testing his strength on the **Mighty Hammer Game**.

I'LL SHOW YOU ALL HOW STRONG I AM! GRRRR!

It was no surprise at all that Blake's hit reached **'MUSCLE MAN'!**

I ALREADY KNEW THAT!

And then Jenny had a go. She swung the
hammer high, then . . .

THUMP!

The machine went **wild!**

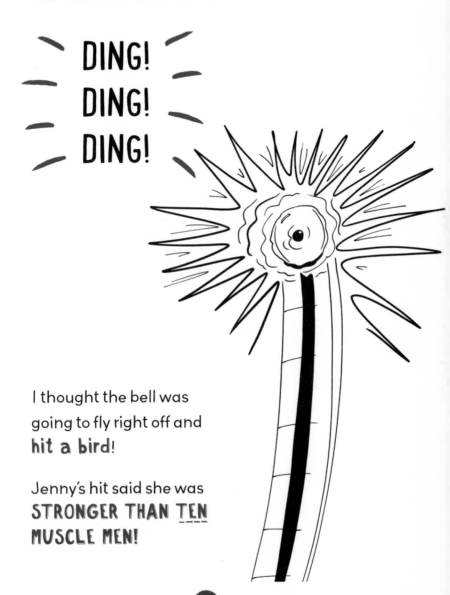

DING!
DING!
DING!

I thought the bell was
going to fly right off and
hit a bird!

Jenny's hit said she was
STRONGER THAN TEN
MUSCLE MEN!

Henry and Hans were playing the **Magnet Game.** I really wanted to have a go too...

But I was worried about my braces. There was **a lot** of metal in my mouth. What if the magnets didn't know which way to go?

What if they all wound up **on my face**? ▶

A

B Fold line B over to meet line A

ZING

I spotted Bella again. She was over at the **Ring Toss**. You had to land a ring over a bottle to win a prize.

I could see **exactly** what she wanted to win...

BIG FROG
PRIZE!

Bella made some **really** good throws ... but she **just** missed the bottles.

She turned and saw me.

WEIR! WEIR!

˙,Oh no!

I quickly turned and **ran away**! I saw a dark doorway and headed straight for it.

It was **really dark** in there and filled with cobwebs.

I could hear wolves **howling** and owls **hooting**, and there was this weird, spooky music coming from somewhere.

Then when I turned a corner, everything went really quiet ... and dark!

I couldn't **hear** a thing!

I couldn't **see** a thing, either!

What was going on?

'Is anybody there?' I called, trembling.

Suddenly something touched me on the shoulder!

I screamed!

EEEEEEEEEEEEEEEEEEEEEEE
EEEEEEEEEEEEEEEEEEEEEEE
EEEEEEEEEEEEEEEEEEEEEEE
EEEEEEEEEEEEEEEEEEEEEEE
EEEEEEEEEEEEEEEEEEEEEEE

EEEEEEEEEEEEEEEEEEEEEEEEEEEEEE
3333333333333333333333333333
EEEEEEEEEEEEEEEEEEEEE
EEEEEEEEEEEEEEEEEEEEEE
3333333333333333333333333
EEEEEEEEEEEEEEEEEEEEE
EEEEEEEEEEEEEEEEEEEEEEEE
3333333333333333333333333
EEEEEEEEEEEEEEEEEK!

Then I heard a **high-pitched** scream right next to me.

EEEEEEEEEEEEEEEEEEEEE
EEEEEEEEEEEEEEEEEEEEEE
EEEEEEEEEEEEEEEEEEEEEE
EEEEEEEEEEEEEEEEEEEEEE
EEEEEEEEEEEEEEEEEEEEEE
EEEEEEEEEEEEEEEEEEEEEE
EEEEEEEEEEEEEEEEEEEEEE
EEEEEEEEEEEEEEEEEEEEEE

EEEEEEEEEEEEEEEEEEEEEEEEEEEEEE
EEEEEEEEEEEEEEEEEEEEEEEEEE
EEEEEEEEEEEEEEEEEEEEEEEEE
EEEEEEEEEEEEEEEEEEEEEEE
EEEEEEEEEEEEEEEEEEEEEEEE
EEEEEEEEEEEEEEEEEEEEEEEEEEEEEE

Bella?

We grabbed each other and hugged **really tight**! Bella was **so** scared I could hear her teeth chattering!

K!

Together, we slowly shuffled out of there and...

...into the daylight.

Phew.

HANS?!   WEIR?!

Huh?

I'd thought **Hans** was **Bella**!

I quickly covered my mouth and laughed.

CHAPTER 5

I found Henry again over at the **Apple** **Bobbing** **Contest.**

HMMMM . . . .

Whoever bobbed and grabbed **the most** apples with their teeth, in the time limit, was the **winner**!

Maybe Henry's pigeon moves would come in handy!

COO! COO! COO!

Just as I was wondering whether I should try the game too, I saw something that made my mind up for me.

The Big Frog Prize!

I lined up next to Henry and some other kids.

WIN ME!

BOBBERS READY?

ON YOUR MARKS, GET SET, GO!

I **splashed** my face right into the water and started **biting** around like a <u>**crazy shark**</u>!

And it turns out my **braces** were a MASSIVE help! I gripped those apples and flung them out, one after the other!

One time, I even managed to get **two** apples in one go! Not only were my braces helping me, but it turns out opening my mouth really wide at the dentist was great **training for apple bobbing**, too!

BZZZZZZZZZZZ

The buzzer went off and we all looked up.

ZZZZZZZ!

My basket was **full**!

WE HAVE A
WINNER!

I'd **won**! And I knew **exactly** what I wanted
for my prize!

It was almost time to get on the bus back to school, but I couldn't find Bella **anywhere**.

Miss Franklin told me that Bella's mum had picked her up early.

'Don't worry, Weir. She'll be back at school tomorrow,' said Miss Franklin.

The **frog** would have to wait until then.

CHAPTER 6

After the Fair, my family was having dinner at the O'Henry's place.

Mrs O'Henry's cooking always **looks awesome**, but **tastes really bad** ... so I was glad we'd ordered **pizza**!

Everyone loves **pizza**.

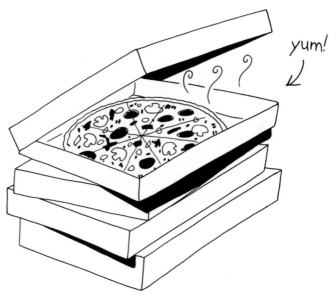

yum!

It was yum, even though big bits of food kept getting stuck in my braces...

STUCK!

The O'Henrys get along **really well** with my family.

Our parents are always joking around . . .

MUSHROOMS ARE GREAT FOR MAKING EARPLUGS!

Sally and Henry's sister, Jane, are always having **boring** conversations...

Roger and the twins like to **dance** together...

And even our pets, Blockhead, FiDo and Mo, love playing together!

YEEHAH!

WOOF! WOOF!

It didn't seem like Blockhead and FiDo were as frightened of me and my braces anymore, but they were **still** keeping away from me.

Henry sat at the dinner table and pretended to be a carnival clown, while Roger stuck leftovers into his mouth.

Everyone laughed.

It was **really funny**, but a couple of things were on my mind. I couldn't stop thinking about Bella—I hadn't spoken to her **all day**.
In fact, I'd avoided her because I didn't want her to see me and my braces.

Would it be **so bad** if she saw them?

Plus, I still had stuff **stuck** in my teeth! It just didn't want to come out!

COME ON!

'Cheer up, Weir,' said Mr O'Henry. 'I get food stuck in my moustache all the time.'

SEE? JUST THINK OF ALL THOSE STUCK BITS AS DESSERT! YUM!

HAHAHAHAA!

Everyone laughed, including me.

'I reckon braces are **cool**,' said Henry. 'Better than having a **giant red pimple** on the end of your nose like I had <u>**all**</u> **day long**.'

'GIANT red pimple?!' I said. 'You can hardly see it!'

'Yeah, I guess it's not **that bad**,' said Henry.

Wow! I wasn't the only one who thought they looked strange. I guess everyone has something about themselves they worry about too much.

Maybe even **Hans Some**.

OH NO! HAIR NUMBER 157 IS OUT OF PLACE!

Then I remembered what my dad said yesterday about laughing and playing along.

So I stood up and smiled.

'You know what?' I said. 'I'm **proud** of my train tracks!'

ALL ABOARD! CHUGGA-CHUGGA CHUGGA-CHUGGA, CHEW, CHEW!

That made **everyone** laugh.

And even better than that . . .

Blockhead and FiDo seemed to think it was
funny, too. They both came over for a cuddle.

Maybe they'd been keeping away from me because I hadn't been **laughing** and **smiling** like my usual self. Maybe it had nothing to do with how I looked with my braces!

SMILE!

CHAPTER 7

I went to school the next day feeling **heaps better** about my braces. They weren't so bad after all.

I spent the whole morning trying to get Bella's attention.

I really needed to explain to her why I'd acted so weird (well, weirder than normal) at the Fair.

It seemed like __she was avoiding me__ now!

Oh man.

It wasn't until the **end** of the day that I finally spoke to her.

BELLA, PLEASE, WAIT!

I had to move faster than Dad at a disco to catch her.

'Bella,' I said, 'I'm really sorry I was kind of avoiding you at the Fair yesterday ... It's just that ... I just got **new braces** ... and I scared the pets ... and I thought maybe you wouldn't like them.'

SEE?

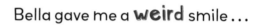

Bella gave me a **weird** smile ...

Did that mean she thought my braces were okay?

I finally gave her the **big** frog.

HERE, I WON THIS FOR YOU YESTERDAY.

'You'd left the Fair before I could give it to you,'
I said.

Bella gave me another smile, but it was still a really **strange** smile.

She looked down and mumbled something. I think she said, 'Thanks, Weir, I love it! I have something to show you, too.'

TO SHOW ME? WHAT IS IT?

And then Bella gave me her **biggest smile** yet!

And guess what?

She had **braces**, too!

'I got them yesterday!' she said. 'That's why I had to leave early. To go to the dentist!'

Ha! Now we **both** had braces!

Bella held up the frog.

She took out a big black pen and drew
something on the frog.

'There, that's better,' she said.

Much better.

FROM ANH

AND JULES

For all our readers, especially the WEIRD ones!

ACKNOWLEDGEMENTS

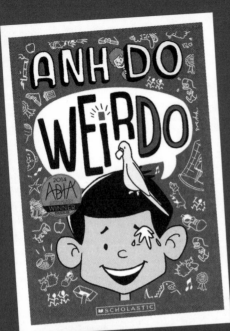

Book 1

GOT IT!

Book 2

GOT IT!

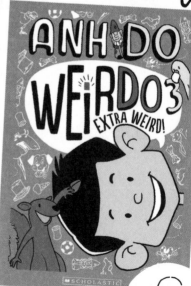

Book 3

GOT IT!

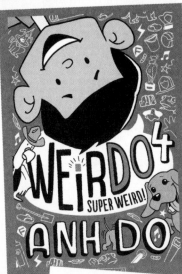

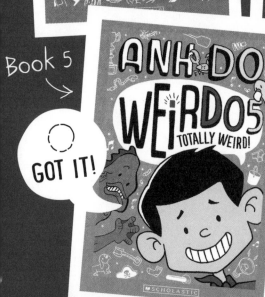
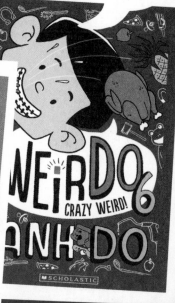

STAY
TUNED!